To my daughter, Sarah, the original SugarLoaf

Atheneum Books for Young Readers

An imprint of Simon & Schuster Children's Publishing Division

1230 Avenue of the Americas

New York, New York 10020

Copyright © 2006 by Peter H. Reynolds

Book design by Lee Wade

The text for this book is set in Aunt Mildred.

The illustrations for this book are rendered in watercolor.

Manufactured in the United States of America

2 4 6 8 10 9 7 5 3

Library of Congress Cataloging-in-Publication Data

Reynolds, Peter H., 1961-.

My very big little world/ Peter H. Reynolds.—1st ed.

p.   cm.

Summary: SugarLoaf, named by her baker father and dentist mother, tells us about her family,

her neighborhood, and what she likes to do.

ISBN-13: 978-0-689-87621-9

ISBN-10: 0-689-87621-1

[1. Family life—Fiction. 2. Day—Fiction.]

PZ7.R337645 Su 2005

[E]—dc22   2004030705

My Very Big Little World

A SUGARLOAF BOOK

written and illustrated by Peter H. Reynolds

Atheneum Books for Young Readers
New York London Toronto Sydney

My name is SugarLoaf.
I didn't name myself.
My mom and dad did.

My mom says that
when I was born,
I looked as sweet as sugar.

Dad says that when
he held me in his arms,
I felt as warm as a
freshly baked loaf of bread.

SugarLoaf—that's me.

I am not the biggest
or the smallest in my family.
My brother is really big.
My sister is really small.
I'm right in the middle.

My big brother's name is Spoke.
My parents named him too.
He is very clever.

SugarLump is my baby sister.

I helped name her.

She makes lots of noise.

I used to talk baby talk, so

I understand her.

I get up early.
So does Dad.

We are morning people.

My dad is a baker.
He makes lots of bread.

He says bread tastes better when I help.

My dad goes to work in a truck.
It's very BIG. I'm smaller.

The truck won't grow. But I will.

Mom wakes up after Dad goes to work.
She likes tea with her newspaper.

I like tea with my friends.

My mom is a dentist for boys and girls.
I'm growing teeth for her to take care of.

She loves it when I brush my teeth.
So does my kitten, Floss.

I draw a lot.
I use my favorite color.
It's Gramma's favorite color too.

Portraits are my specialty.
SugarLump helps.

Collages are fun.

Mom hangs them in our gallery.

I love my neighborhood.
It has tall trees and cozy houses.
People in my neighborhood like music.

I play drums for them.

Some days are extra special.
Aunt Cabby comes to visit.

I give her advice.

When she goes back to work,

I go back to work too.

Then I need a nap.

There is an ocean near my house. It is very big.
The puddles in my yard are very small
but good to sail boats in.

Outside is one of my favorite places.
There are bugs and birds there.

Birds think
I'm a bird.

The sky is very, very, very big.
The stars are very, very, very small.

But mom told me that stars are
actually quite big.
She says faraway things look small.

Some things are big and small
at the same time.

Like me!

See you next time.

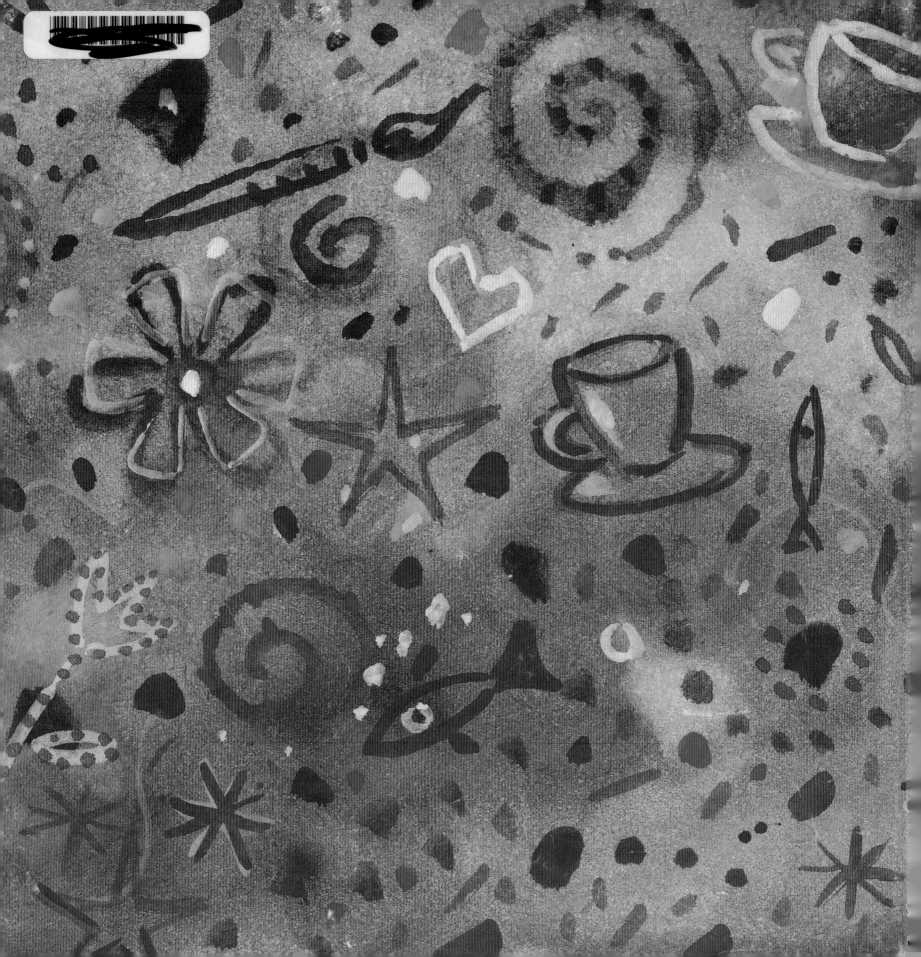